DATE DUE

The Wishing Club

a story about fractions

Donna Jo Napoli ✳ pictures by Anna Currey

HENRY HOLT AND COMPANY
NEW YORK

Henry Holt and Company, LLC
Publishers since 1866
175 Fifth Avenue
New York, New York 10010
www.henryholtchildrensbooks.com

Henry Holt® is a registered trademark of Henry Holt and Company, LLC.
Text copyright © 2007 by Donna Jo Napoli
Illustrations copyright © 2007 by Anna Currey
All rights reserved.
Distributed in Canada by H. B. Fenn and Company Ltd.

Library of Congress Cataloging-in-Publication Data
Napoli, Donna Jo.
The Wishing Club: a story about fractions / Donna Jo Napoli;
illustrated by Anna Currey.—1st ed.
p. cm.
Summary: When four siblings wish on a star, each gets only
a fraction of what he or she wanted, but when they combine
their wishes, they just might get a whole new pet.
ISBN-13: 978-0-8050-7665-3 / ISBN-10: 0-8050-7665-4
[1. Wishes—Fiction. 2. Brothers and sisters—Fiction. 3. Fractions—
Fiction.] I. Currey, Anna, ill. II. Title. III. Title: Story about fractions.
PZ7.N15Wis 2007   [E]—dc22   2006030767

First Edition—2007 / Designed by Amelia May Anderson
Printed in the United States of America on acid-free paper. ∞

1 3 5 7 9 10 8 6 4 2

*To all teachers who instill a love of numbers in their students
(but especially to the spirit of Mrs. JoAnne Taber)*

—D. J. N.

For Robert, with love

—A. C.

Petey and Joey stood on the porch looking up at the night sky.

"What're you doing?" asked Sally.

"Wishing on a star," said Petey, who was four.

"Star," said Joey.

Sally moved closer to Petey. "So, what are you wishing for?"

"A dollar," said Petey.

"Dollar," said Joey. Joey was only two, and it was way past his bedtime.

Sally was eight and knew everything. "That's goofy. Let's all go to bed."

The next night the kids were back outside.

"Are you wishing again?" asked Sally.

"It worked last night," said Petey. "Look."

"That's not a dollar. That's a quarter. You need four of those to make a dollar."

Petey put the quarter in his pocket. "Well, then, I'll wish again."

"Me, too," said Joey.

"You want to wish, Joey?" asked Sally. "What for?"

"Cookie."

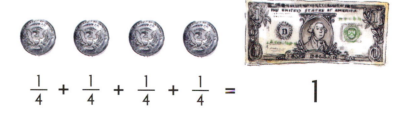

$$\frac{1}{4} + \frac{1}{4} + \frac{1}{4} + \frac{1}{4} = \quad 1$$

It takes 4 quarters to make 1 dollar.

Petey has $\frac{1}{4}$ of a dollar.

The following night Sally peeked out the door.
"I can't believe it. You're at it again?"

Petey held out his hand. "Got another quarter."

Joey held out his hand. "Cookie."

Sally frowned. "That's only half a cookie."

"That's what Mamma had left in the bag," said Petey. "Half a cookie. And she gave it to Joey." He looked up at the sky. "It's a good wishing star."

"It's a weird wishing star," said Sally. "It doesn't work right."

$$\frac{1}{2} \quad + \quad \frac{1}{2} \quad = \quad 1$$

It takes 2 half cookies to make 1 whole cookie. Joey has $\frac{1}{2}$ of a cookie.

"Hey, what's up?" Samantha, Sally's twin, came out onto the porch. "I've seen you out here three nights in a row."

Petey pointed. "We're wishing on our lucky star."

"But they never get what they wish for," said Sally.

"Yes, we do," said Petey. "Only not all of it."

"Joey wishes for a cookie and he gets half a cookie," said Sally. "Petey wishes for a dollar and he gets a quarter."

"You're wishing wrong," said Samantha.

"Like you know!" said Sally.

Petey tugged on Samantha's shirt. "How do you wish right?"

"Like this: 'Star light, star bright, first star I see tonight—'"

"But it's not the first star," said Petey.

"That's just how it goes, Petey. Then you say, 'I wish I may, I wish I might, get the wish I wish tonight.' "

"Okay," said Petey. "I'm going to wish."

"Let's all wish," said Samantha. "What do you want, Sally?"

"You'll see."

The four of them gathered outside at twilight.

"What'd you get from last night's wishes?" asked Samantha.

Petey held out his hand. "Another quarter."

Joey held out his hand. "Cookie."

"That's only half a cookie," said Sally.

"You didn't get what you wished for either, did you?" said Petey.

"Actually, I did." Sally emptied her pocket.

"Marbles." Petey counted them. "Wow. Ten of them."

"But I didn't get a full bag," said Sally. "The label says eighty marbles."

"Ten's good, though," said Petey.

"Good," said Joey.

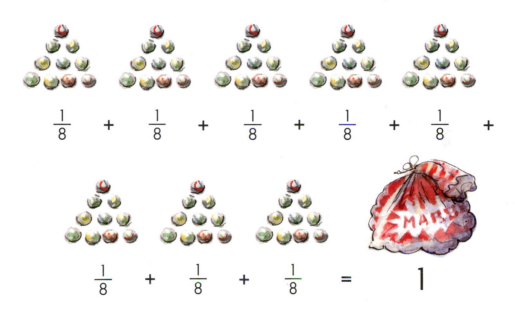

$$\frac{1}{8} + \frac{1}{8} + \frac{1}{8} + \frac{1}{8} + \frac{1}{8} +$$

$$\frac{1}{8} + \frac{1}{8} + \frac{1}{8} = 1$$

It takes 8 groups of 10 marbles to make a full bag. Sally has $\frac{1}{8}$ of a full bag of marbles.

"Ten's a lot less than eighty," said Sally. "What did you wish for, Samantha?"

"You're not going to believe this." Samantha pulled a bag out of her pocket. The label said eighty marbles, but it wasn't full. "Guess how many marbles are here?"

"Ten," said Sally.

They all looked up at the sky.

"What's going on?" whispered Samantha.

"Let's all wish again," said Petey.

"You know," said Samantha as they stood in a circle, "we ought to form a club. The Wishing Club."

"Everyone hold out what you got," said Sally.

"Another half cookie," said Samantha. "Another quarter. And two more bags with only ten marbles."

"Yuck," said Sally.

"But now I have four quarters," said Petey. "And that makes a dollar. And a dollar is all I need."

"Cookie good," said Joey.

Sally sighed. "You guys don't get it. You're not supposed to be happy with less than what you wished for. There's something wrong."

"Hey, I think I've got it," said Samantha.

"Got what?" asked Petey.

"The pattern. Joey is two. And when he wishes, he gets half of what he wants. Petey is four. And when he wishes, he gets one fourth of what he wants. Sally's eight, like me. And when we wish, we get one eighth of what we want."

"What are you talking about?" said Petey.

"Our star is special," said Sally.

"Star," said Joey.

"Daddy said it's not a star," said Samantha. "It's a comet. And this is the last night it will be visible for years and years."

"Then I'm going to wish for a million marbles," said Sally.

"Don't be dumb," said Samantha. "Wish for something good."

"You wished for marbles, too. If I'm dumb, so are you," said Sally.

"Okay, we were both dumb. But let's be smart now. Let's wish for something we really want."

"A dinosaur," said Petey.

Sally groaned. "If you wish for a dinosaur, Petey, you'll only get a quarter of it. Gross."

"Pig," said Joey.

Everyone looked at Joey.

"I've always wanted a little pig," said Samantha.

"Me, too," said Sally.

Petey nodded. "But I don't want a quarter of a pig."

"Maybe we could get a whole pig," said Sally. "If we all wished for the same thing."

$$\frac{1}{2} + \frac{1}{4} + \frac{1}{8} + \frac{1}{8} = 1$$

"If Joey wished for a pig, he'd get half," said
Samantha. "And if Petey wished, he'd get a quarter.
And if we twins wished, we'd each get an eighth. I think
that adds up to a whole pig, right?"

"We have to be sure about this," said Sally. "Too much is at stake. Come on." She led the way into the kitchen and took out the measuring cups.

Sally handed Joey the half cup and Petey the quarter cup. "Fill them with water and pour them into the whole cup."

"I'm using mustard," said Petey. "It looks better."

"Ketchup," said Joey. "Red."

So Joey and Petey poured mustard and ketchup into the whole cup.

"Now I'll add an eighth cup of soy sauce," said Sally.

"That's all the spicy toppings we have," said Samantha. "So I'll add an eighth cup of maple syrup," and she did.

The cup was full.

$$\frac{1}{2} + \frac{1}{4} + \frac{1}{8} + \frac{1}{8} = 1$$

The kids went back out to the porch in silence.
They wished on the comet.

In the morning, Mamma said, "I have a surprise for you kids."

"Pig," said Joey.

Mamma gaped. "Who told you?"

"A comet," said Petey.

"Is it missing anything?" asked Sally. "Any parts?"

"What?" said Mamma.

"Just show us," said Petey.

Mamma opened the door. In trotted a very small pig.

"It's got two ears," said Samantha. "And four legs and everything a pig needs—even a tail."

"A curly tail," said Petey.

"A corkscrew tail," said Sally.

"Corkscrew," said Joey.

So that's what they called him:
Corkscrew. And he was all pig.

Dear Readers, Big and Small,

✳

Why would it be great, but maybe mathematically uninteresting, if there was someone in the family who was only one year old, but who could speak well enough to wish on this magic comet?

✳

Ask what would happen in this situation if the family had children of different ages who wished on this magic comet. For example, if there were two children in the family, and one was five and the other was ten, and both wished for a dollar, how much would each child get? What if the family had three children, ages three, six, and twelve, and they wished for a bag of sixty marbles—how many marbles would each child get?

✳

So long as the children wished for an animal, we needed twin eight-year-olds in this story. Why? Can you think of any combination of ages for children in a family that would have allowed them to wish for an animal and get a complete animal without there being any twins or triplets or quadruplets (or quintuplets, or . . .)?

✳

Try seeing how many different ways you can divide up a given number. For example, put eighty marbles in a bowl. Divide them into equal groups eight different ways. Now try it with one hundred marbles in the bowl.

✳

Explain why in America it makes sense for us to have pennies, nickels, dimes, quarters, half dollars, and dollar coins. Why don't we have a coin worth fifteen cents, for example? Why don't we have a coin worth twenty-one cents? Is there any value for a coin that you might have expected but that is missing?